FIELD TRIP TO FLYING FEATHERS FARM

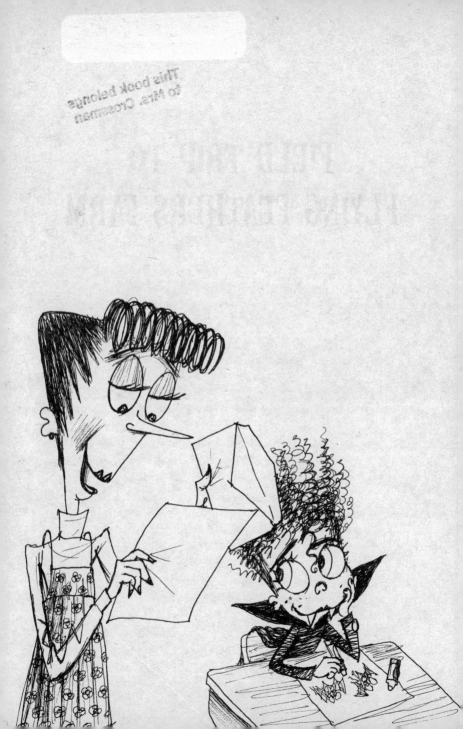

FIELD TRIP TO FLYING FEATHERS FARM

BY MICHELLE POPLOFF
ILLUSTRATED BY BILL BASSO

SCHOLASTIC INC.

New York   Toronto   London   Auckland   Sydney

Mexico City   New Delhi   Hong Kong   Buenos Aires

Happy Birthday, Dad
Love, Shainee Pickle.

For Joe Toto
—B. B.

ISBN-13: 978-0-439-27618-4
ISBN-10: 0-439-27618-7

Text copyright © 2002 by Michelle Poploff.
Illustrations copyright © 2002 by Bill Basso.
All rights reserved. Published by Scholastic Inc.
SCHOLASTIC and associated logos are trademarks and/or
registered trademarks of Scholastic Inc.

12 11 10 9 8 7 6 5 4 3 2   8 9 10 11 12/0

Printed in the U.S.A.   40
First printing, October 2002

CONTENTS

Chapter 1
FIELD TRIP FUN

Br-ring, br-ring!

The sound of the school bell filled
Mrs. Bono's classroom.

The children quieted down as Mrs. Bono
held up a letter.

"I have good news," she said. "I received
a letter from Wayne Dobbs's grandfather.
He's invited us on a field trip to his farm."

"All right!" the class shouted.

The kids closest to Wayne slapped him
high fives.

A small, secret bell went off in Wanda Doomsday's head.

She had always wanted to go to a farm, for a very special reason.

She turned to Wayne the Pain Dobbs.

"Does your grandpa have a barn with horses and cows?" she asked.

Wayne nodded.

"And he has some pigs, chickens, and sheep. My grandpa's farm is the best," he said, thumping his chest.

"Can we milk some cows?" asked Hector.

"Milking a cow is no big deal," said Wanda.

"Have you ever tried it?" asked Wayne.

"I will at the farm," said Wanda. "You'll see."

"Let's remember our manners," said Mrs. Bono. "We'll be Farmer Dobbs's guests. He'll show us around, and we'll see where some of our food comes from."

Mrs. Bono looked at her trip chart. "Wanda, your grandmother is next on our list of class helpers. Do you think she'd like to join us?"

"Sure," said Wanda. "Granny loves nature."

That should show that hotshot Wayne, she thought. *All the kids have fun when my Granny Doomsday is around.*

"Good," said Mrs. Bono. "Before our trip, I want everyone to read about different farm animals. Let's see what we can collect and bring back from our field trip."

Wanda Doomsday knew exactly what she wanted to bring back.

And whatever Wanda wanted, Wanda usually got.

Chapter 2
FLYING FEATHERS FARM

Farmer Dobbs was at his front gate
when the class got off the bus.
"Welcome to Flying Feathers Farm,"
he said.
Wayne ran over and hugged his grandpa.
"Come on out back and I'll show you
around," Farmer Dobbs said. "First stop
is the pigpen. Who wants to hold a
piglet?"
"I do!" said Helen.

When Farmer Dobbs handed the piglet
to Helen, it squealed so much she put
it down.

"His skin felt rough," she said.

Farmer Dobbs nodded.

"Do you know anything else about pigs?"
he asked.

"They hunt for food by digging in
the dirt with their noses," said Hector.

14

He and Wayne made piggy noises
at each other.

"They roll in the mud to keep cool,"
added Wanda.

"Very good," said Farmer Dobbs.

"Hey, Wanda," said Wayne. "What
do you call a dancing pig?"

"What?" asked Wanda.

"Shakin' bacon," said Wayne.

Everyone laughed.

15

"How did they catch the crooks at
the pig farm?" Wanda asked.

Wayne shrugged.

"Someone squealed!" shouted Wanda.

"I haven't heard that one before,"
said Farmer Dobbs.

Wanda giggled.

She liked farm funnies.

Holding tightly to the shoe box she had
brought with her, she followed the farmer.

"Would you like to put that down?"
Farmer Dobbs asked.

"No, thanks," Wanda said. "I may be
needing it soon."

Next they passed some sheep.

"I just love their woolly coats," said Buffy.

"Do your lambs get lots of exercise?"

"Oh, yes," said Farmer Dobbs. "We keep them in *sheep shape*."

The class laughed.

"That is so *ba-aad*, Grandpa," said Wayne.

Farmer Dobbs put his arm around
Wayne's shoulder.

"Now gather 'round and meet some
more of our farm family," he said.

"Over in the back is our big rooster.
And those hens in the corner are sitting
on their eggs to keep them warm."

The class tossed chicken feed into the
pens.

Feathers flew as the chicks and hens
wobbled over.

"Oh, Farmer Dobbs," said Granny
Doomsday. "Did you hear about the
naughty rooster?"

"Why, no, ma'am," he said.

"He flew the coop!" said Granny.

"Way to go, Granny," said Wanda with
a laugh.

"What did the rooster say to the hen?"
Farmer Dobbs asked Granny Doomsday.

"Don't know," she said.

"You're *eggs*-actly my type."

Granny giggled.

"That's a good *yolk*," she said.

Chapter 3
THE MILKING LESSON

Inside the barn, Wanda clutched her
box closer.

She walked slowly, looking all around.

"*Moo*-ve it, Wanda," said Hector,
bumping into her.

"*Moo* to you, too," Wanda shot back.

"Now you'll see a farmer in action,"
said Farmer Dobbs, entering the barn.
While the kids crowded around the
cow stall, he sat on a wooden stool
and showed them how to milk a cow.

The milk fell into a tin bucket, making a plinking sound.

Wanda paid no attention to the milking lesson.

She was too busy looking around the barn for something else.

"Who wants to try?" asked Farmer Dobbs.

Suddenly, Wanda remembered her boast about milking a cow.

"I'll do it," she said, pushing past the others.

Wanda looked right at Wayne.

"Milking a cow is easy," she said.

"Now, remember what I said," Farmer Dobbs began.

"I do, I do," Wanda said quickly.

She sat on the stool and began milking.

"See," she said, turning to Wayne,
"it's easy —"
That's when the milk squirted her
smack in the eye.
"Yikes!" cried Wanda.
"Ha-ha-ha! Easy!" said Wayne.
Farmer Dobbs handed Wanda a
handkerchief.
"That happens to lots of first timers,"
he said. "Right, Wayne?"
Wayne stopped laughing.
"Guess so," he mumbled.

Just then a bell rang.

Granny hugged Wanda.

"Saved by the bell, dearie," she said.

"Lunchtime!" called Farmer Dobbs.

"Let's see what my helper, Bub, has

cooked up."

Wanda was hungry, but she wanted

to check around the barn some more.

Her search would have to wait.

Chapter 4
CHOW TIME

"Chow time!" Bub called.

Everyone washed up at the big outdoor sinks.

Bub was cooking hamburgers and hot dogs over an open grill.

"That smells great," said Hector.

"Will the hamburgers be long?"

"No," said Wanda, "they'll be *round*."

"Knock, knock," said Wayne.

"Who's there?" asked Bub.

"Gorilla."

"Gorilla who?"

"Gorilla me a hamburger, please,"
said Wayne.

"Coming right up," said Bub.

Granny turned to Farmer Dobbs.
"Make sure you save room for my
booberry pie."
She passed out slices to everyone.
Bub took a big bite and grinned.
"Why didn't the skeleton come on
your field trip?" he asked.
"Why?" asked Granny.
"Because he had no *body* to go with."
"That's a good one for Halloween,"
said Helen.
She looked down at the grass.
"There sure are lots of ants at this
picnic," she said.
"Plenty of ants, but no
uncles," said Hector.

28

"Uh-oh," said Wayne, beginning to squirm. "I think I have some ants in my pants. Maybe that's what I'll bring back to class."

"These bugs are driving me batty,"
said Buffy. "Shoo, fly, shoo! Now,
what's this fly doing in my ghoulade?"
Wanda looked into the drink.
"Looks like the backstroke to me, Buff."
"Ouch!" said Hector, slapping his nose.
He began scratching.
"Looks like a bug bite," said Buffy. "You
can bring that back to class."
"Ha-ha!" laughed Wayne. "Look at
that big red bump on Hector's nose."

Hector began chasing Wayne around
in a circle.
"Whoops!" yelled Wayne.
The boys slipped and landed in a
pool of mud.

"Slime time!" Wayne shouted.

"They look like those little piggies playing in the mud," said Helen.

"That's enough, boys," called Mrs. Bono. Both boys' jeans were covered with the muddy slime.

"We'll bring these to class," Hector said proudly.

"That's *not* what I had in mind for our field trip collection," said Mrs. Bono.

"Come inside and clean up," said Bub.

"I'll look for different leaves to bring to class," said Helen. "Lots of leaves."

"Good idea," said Mrs. Bono, looking relieved.

Chapter 5
WHAT WANDA WANTS

Helen asked Wanda if she'd like to help look for leaves.

"No, thanks. I have another idea," Wanda said, walking over to Farmer Dobbs.

"Do you have any bats in the barn?"

Farmer Dobbs scratched his chin.

"You're in luck, young lady. I do have an old bat in the barn. Would you like it?"

"Oh, yes, sir, I would!" Wanda said, jumping up and down. "That's what I want to bring back from our field trip."

She was hoping for a baby bat, but an old bat would have to do.

Farmer Dobbs went into the barn
and came out with an old wooden
baseball bat.

Wanda's eyes opened wide.

"Oh, no, I didn't mean that kind of bat.
Don't you have any black bats sleeping
in your barn?"

"I'm sorry, but right now I don't have
any of those bats," said Farmer Dobbs.
"But I could surely use some to get rid of
these pesky insects."

"Bats are disgusting," said Buffy.

"No, they're not," said Wanda. "I read
all about them. They help farmers by
eating the bugs that ruin the crops.
They're cute and gentle, and they even
hang upside down."

When Wanda finished, she sighed. *Now I have nothing for the field trip collection*, she thought.

"Wait! I've got it!" said Farmer Dobbs. He went back into the barn and brought out an old wooden box.

"We used this bat house years ago," he said. "It's still in fine shape inside and out. Hang it high in a tree where it will get some sun. Maybe a bat will fly into your neck of the woods some night."

"Don't call me if it does," said Buffy.

"Don't worry, I won't," said Wanda. "But I will call you, Farmer Dobbs. Thank you very much."

Turning to her teacher, Wanda said,
"Isn't this great, Mrs. Bono?"
"It certainly is different, Wanda," Mrs.
Bono said. "Just like you. What else
have we collected?"

"Lots of leaves," said Helen.

"I have a snip of wool from a sheep,"
said Buffy.

"I have ants in my muddy pants,"
said Wayne.

"A bug bite and jeans with pond
slime," said Hector.

"Let's stop right there," said Mrs. Bono,
laughing. "Here's our bus."

Chapter 6
FAREWELL TO THE FARM

Before leaving, the class helped gather
farm-fresh eggs to take home.
"The day has gone by so quickly,"
said Mrs. Bono. "I wish we could have
seen and done more."
"Why not come back again for
pumpkins?" asked Farmer Dobbs.

"Granny makes the best pumpkin pie ever," said Wanda.

"That settles it! You'll have to come pick some pumpkins for your pies," said Farmer Dobbs, shaking Granny's hand.

"It's a date," said Granny.

A DATE!

Wanda and Wayne stared at each other. Wanda sprang into action.

"Time to get back on the ghoul bus, Granny," she said, tugging on her grandmother's arm.

Granny smiled at Farmer Dobbs.

"When you come to town, do drop in at the Doomsdays' and join me in a glass of my special bubbly brew."

"Join you in a glass?" Farmer Dobbs joked. "Will there be enough room in there for the two of us?"

"Oh, brother," said Wayne. "We really have to go, Grandpa. I'll see you soon."

"Thanks for everything!" the kids shouted.

Bub rode up on Farmer Dobbs's horse and waved good-bye.

When everyone was on the bus, Farmer Dobbs called out, "Did you hear about the farmer who went to town on Friday, stayed for two days, and left on Friday? How could that be?"

"We don't know," the kids answered.

Farmer Dobbs pointed to his horse.

"His horse was named Friday," he said.

"We'll see you at pumpkin picking time."